A Giant First-Start Reader

This easy reader contains only 53 different words,
repeated often to help the young reader develop
word recognition and interest in reading.

Basic word list for *You Dirty Dog*

a	he	plays
am	here	says
and	I	*Shhh*
are	if	sleep
bath	in	soap
Benny	is	Sue
Dan	know	the
dirt	like	then
dirty	likes	they
do	me	this
does	mud	water
dust	no	we
feel	not	what
funny	now	who
give	off	will
goes	one	with
good	Penny	you
had	play	

You Dirty Dog

Written by Stephen Caitlin

Illustrated by Debi Hamuka-Falkenham

Troll Associates

Library of Congress Cataloging in Publication Data

Caitlin, Stephen.
   You dirty dog.

   Summary: While Dan the dog takes a nap, his
animal friends give him a bath.
   [1. Cleanliness—Fiction. 2. Dogs—Fiction.
3. Animals—Fiction] I. Hamuka-Falkenham, Debi, ill.
II. Title.
PZ7.C122Yo   1988   [E]   87-19182
ISBN 0-8167-1103-8 (lib. bdg.)
ISBN 0-8167-1104-6 (pbk.)

10 9 8 7 6 5 4 3 2

This is Dan.
Do you know what Dan likes?

He likes dirt . . .
and dust . . .

and mud.
Dan, you are dirty!

Do you know what Dan does *not* like?
He does not like soap.

He does not like water.
Dan does not like a bath.

Dirty Dan says, "I will play.
Who will play with me?"

"Will you play in the dirt?" says Dan.
"Not me," says Sue.

"Will you play in the dust?" says Dan.
"Not me," says Benny.

"Will you play in the mud?" says Dan.
"Not me," says Penny.

"This is *not* funny," says Dan.
"No one will play."

"If no one will play, I will sleep."
Off goes Dan.

Off he goes to sleep.

Shhh!
Here is Sue.

Shhh!
Here is Benny.

Shhh!
Here is Penny.

Do you know what Sue and Benny
and Penny will do?

They will give Dan a bath!

"*Shhh!*" says Sue.

"This is funny," says Dan.
"I am not dirty—and I feel good!"

"Dan," says Sue.
"You had a bath.
Now we will play!"

Now Dan plays in the dirt . . .

and the dust . . .

and the mud.

And then . . .

Dan plays in the bath!